This book belongs to:

. . . .

. . . .

To David and to Lucy
with love

The correspondence in this book is a work of fiction.
The name Greenpeace is used by kind permission of
Greenpeace UK, Canonbury Villas,
London N1 2PN

For more information on
Greenpeace's book campaign
visit www.saveordelete.com

To find out more about
Simon James and his books visit
www.simonjamesbooks.com

First published 1991 by Walker Books Ltd
87 Vauxhall Walk, London SE11 5HJ

This edition published 2008

6 8 10 9 7

© 1991 Simon James

The right of Simon James to be identified as author/illustrator
of this work has been asserted by him in accordance with the
Copyright, Designs and Patents Act 1988

This book has been typeset in Palatino
and handlettered by Simon James

Printed in China

British Library Cataloguing in Publication Data:
a catalogue record for this book is available
from the British Library

ISBN 978-1-4063-0848-8

www.walker.co.uk

SIMON JAMES
Dear Greenpeace

WALKER BOOKS
AND SUBSIDIARIES
LONDON • BOSTON • SYDNEY • AUCKLAND

Dear Greenpeace,

   I love whales very much and
I think I saw one in my pond
today. Please send me some
information on whales, as
I think he might be hurt.

                    Love
                    Emily

Dear Emily,

   Here are some details about whales. I don't think you'll find it was a whale you saw, because whales don't live in ponds, but in salt water.

Yours sincerely,
Greenpeace

Dear Greenpeace,

I am now putting salt into the pond every day before school and last night I saw my whale smile. I think he is feeling better. Do you think he might be lost?

Love
Emily

Dear Emily,

   Please don't put any more salt
in the pond, I'm sure your parents
won't be pleased.

   I'm afraid there can't be a whale
in your pond, because whales don't
get lost, they always know where
they are in the oceans.

Yours sincerely,
Greenpeace

Dear Greenpeace,
   Tonight I am very happy because I saw my whale jump up and spurt lots of water. He looked blue.
   Does this mean he might be a blue whale?

Love
Emily

P.S. What can I feed him with?

Dear Emily,

Blue whales are blue and they eat tiny shrimp-like creatures that live in the sea. However I must tell you that a blue whale is much too big to live in your pond.

Yours sincerely,
Greenpeace

P.S. Perhaps it is a blue goldfish?

Dear Greenpeace,

   Last night I read your letter to my whale. Afterwards he let me stroke his head. It was very exciting.

   I secretly took him some crunched-up cornflakes and bread-crumbs. This morning I looked in the pond and they were all gone!

   I think I shall call him Arthur, what do you think?

Love
Emily

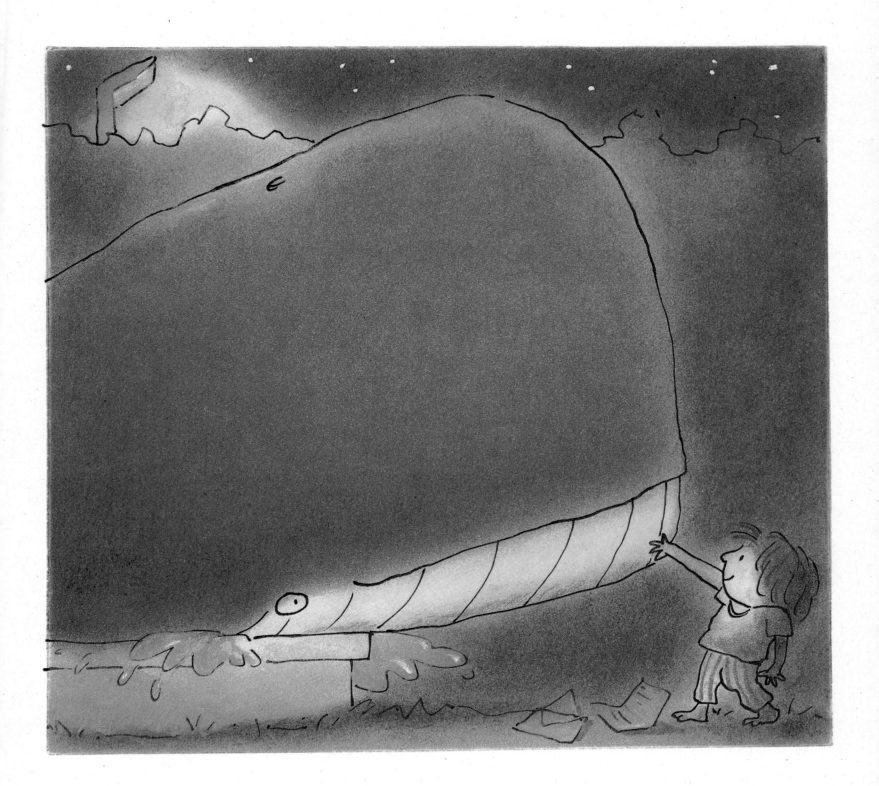

Dear Emily,

I must point out to you quite forcefully now that in no way could a whale live in your pond. You may not know that whales are migratory, which means they travel great distances each day.

I am sorry to disappoint you.

Yours sincerely,
Greenpeace

Dear Greenpeace,
   Tonight I'm a little sad. Arthur
has gone. I think your letter made
sense to him and he has decided
to be migratory again.

                Love
                Emily

Dear Emily,

Please don't be too sad, it really was impossible for a whale to live in your pond. Perhaps when you are older you would like to sail the oceans studying and protecting whales with us.

Yours sincerely,
Greenpeace

Dear Greenpeace,

   It's been the happiest day!
I went to the seaside and you'll
never guess, but I saw Arthur!
I called to him and he smiled.
I knew it was Arthur because
he let me stroke his head.

   I gave him some of my
sandwich...

and then we said goodbye.
I shouted that I loved him very
much and, I hope you don't mind,
I said you loved him too.

love
Emily (and Arthur)

The End

SIMON JAMES

Simon James is an award-winning author and illustrator of books for children – creator of the much-loved character Baby Brains and of touching tales exploring a child's unique relationship with Nature.

ISBN 978-1-84428-522-8

ISBN 978–1-4063-0847-1

ISBN 978-1-4063-0846-4

ISBN 978-1-4063-0848-8

ISBN 978-1-4063-0202-8

ISBN 978–1-4063-0845-7

ISBN 978-1-4063-0849-5

ISBN 978-1-84428-467-2

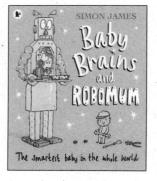

ISBN 978-1-4063-1338-3

"Drawing always opens up a very private and delightful world. It's easy to forget that drawing in itself is a kind of magic. Drawing is good for you!" SIMON JAMES

Available from all good bookstores
www.walker.co.uk